Blippo & Beep

I Feel Funny

For Charlie and Lulu, love Gigi—SW
For Ma and Pa Turner—JE

PENGUIN WORKSHOP
An imprint of Penguin Random House LLC, New York

First published simultaneously in paperback and hardcover in the United States of America
by Penguin Workshop, an imprint of Penguin Random House LLC, New York, 2022

Text copyright © 2022 by Sarah Weeks
Illustrations copyright © 2022 by Joey Ellis

Visit us online at penguinrandomhouse.com.

Library of Congress Cataloging-in-Publication Data is available.

Manufactured in China

ISBN 9780593227008 (hc)   10 9 8 7 6 5 4 3 2 1 TOPL

I Feel Funny

by Sarah Weeks
illustrated by Joey Ellis

Penguin Workshop

9

Beep Feels Funny

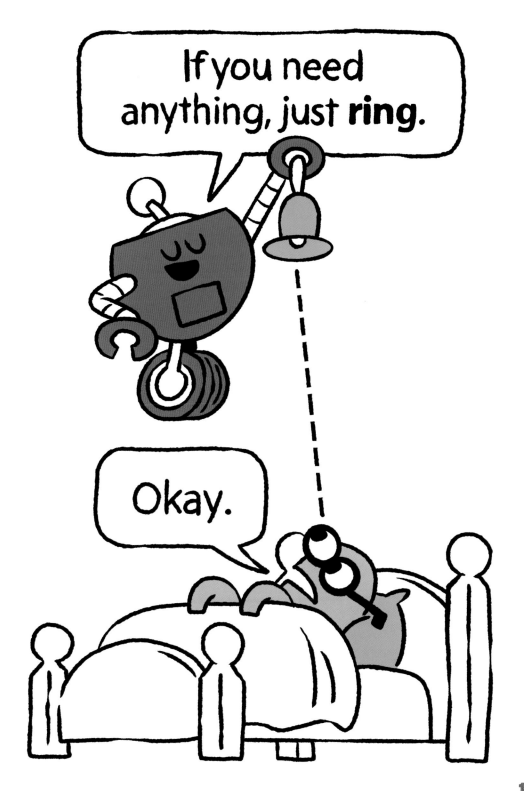

19

26

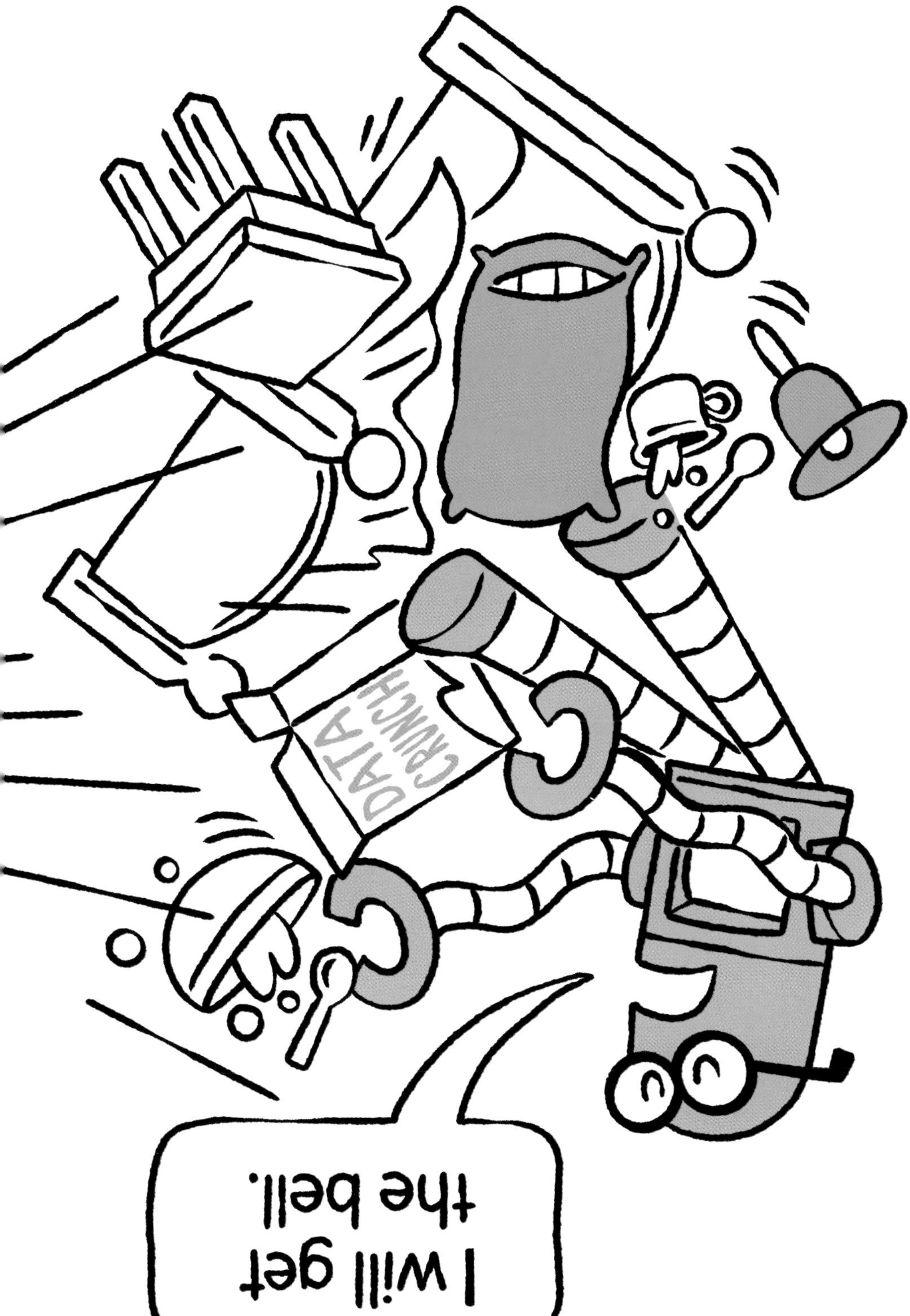
DATA CRUNCH
I will get the bell.

43

47